11.70

j811
ADO

Adoff, Arnold

Black is brown is
tan

103193

3/87

AR
DL 2.9
PtS 0.5

for
Leigh and Jaime
black and tan
kiss big sister
hug young man

Black is brown is tan
Text copyright © 1973 by Arnold Adoff
Illustrations copyright © 1973 by Emily Arnold McCully
information address Harper & Row, Publishers, Inc., 10 East
53rd Street, New York, N.Y. 10022. Published simultaneously
in Canada by Fitzhenry & Whiteside Limited, Toronto.
Library of Congress Catalog Card Number: 72-9855
Trade Standard Book Number: 06-020083-9
Harpercrest Standard Book Number: 06-020084-7

Black
is brown
is tan

by Arnold Adoff

pictures by Emily Arnold McCully

Harper & Row, Publishers

black is brown is tan
is girl is boy
is nose is face
is all the colors
of the race

is dark is light
singing songs
in singing night
kiss big woman hug big man
black is brown is tan

this is the way it is for us   this is the way we are

i am mom am mommy mama mamu meeny muh
 and mom again
with mighty hugs and hairbrush mornings
 catching curls
later we sit by the window
 and your head is up against my chest
we read and tickle and sing the words into the air

go out to cut wood for the fire
or cook the corn and chicken legs

and you say you getting bigger than me
and you say   chocolate momma
chocolate up the milk

and i say drink the milk
and laugh out loud

i am black i am brown the milk is chocolate brown
i am the color of the milk
   chocolate cheeks and hands
that darken in the summer sun a nose
   that peels brown skin in august

i am black
i am a brown sugar gown
a tasty tan and coffee pumpkin pie
with dark brown eyes and almond ears
and my face gets ginger red
when i puff and yell you into bed

this is the way it is for us   this is the way we are

i am dad am daddy dingbat da and kiss me pa
with the big belly and the loud voice
sitting at my desk and you sit on my lap
we read and laugh and pinch the words
  into the air

go out to cut wood for the fire
or cook the corn and hamburgers

and you say you getting bigger than me
when i say drink the milk

i am white   the milk is white   i am not the color
of the milk   i am white   the snow is white   i am not
the color of the snow

i am white   i am white
i am light
with pinks and tiny tans
dark hair growing on my arms
that darken in the summer sun
brown eyes   big yellow ears

and my face gets tomato red
when i puff and yell you into bed

this is the way it is for us   this is the way we are

daddy's sister florence with the gold gold hair
and momma's tan man brother
   who plays the frying pan

there is granny white and grandma black
kissing both your cheeks and hugging back

sitting by the window telling stories of ago

and you say you getting bigger than all of them
and pour a glass of milk for every one

black is brown is tan
is girl is boy
is nose is face
is all the colors
of the race

is dark   is light
singing songs
in singing night

kiss big woman hug big man
black is brown is tan